THE WORST CLASS IN THE WORLD

KT-375-064

DO YOU HAVE THEM ALL?

☐ THE WORST CLASS IN THE WORLD

☐ THE WORST CLASS IN THE WORLD GETS WORSE

☐ THE WORST CLASS IN THE WORLD DARES YOU!

☐ THE WORST CLASS IN THE WORLD GOES WILD!
(That's this one!)

ADD AN EXTRA TICK IF YOU'VE GOT

☐ THE WORST CLASS IN THE WORLD IN DANGER!
THE WORLD BOOK DAY EXCLUSIVE
(Mrs Bottomley-Blunt would be proud!)

ST REGINA'S
CLASS

Mrs Bottomley-Blunt

Headmistress.
Has a long, laminated List of Rules.
Makes a noise like a horse when
she is annoyed, which is a lot.

Mr Nidgett

Teacher of 4B.
Firm believer that
everything can be
mended with kindness.
Often proved wrong.

Stanley Bradshaw

Fond of footling, fiddle-faddling
and shilly-shallying, much to
Mrs Bottomley-Blunt's annoyance.

Manjit Morris

Stanley's best friend.
Determined to be the First Human
Boy ever to do a lot of dangerous,
foolish and impossible things.

Keith Mears

Self-proclaimed King of the Internet.
Falls asleep in class a lot.

Lionel Dawes

Called Lionel, even though she is a girl, because her mum says names do not have genders, they are just words, which is true if you think about it, but Mrs Bottomley-Blunt does not agree.

Bruce Bingley

Once got a plastic brontosaurus stuck up his nose for a week. Can burp the national anthem.

Lacey Braithwaite

Compulsive liar.

Penelope Potts

Muriel Lemon

Knows too many medical facts. Fond of warning Mr Nidgett of the dangers of everything.

Annoying telltale. Identical twin of Hermione Potts in 4A, and determined to join her by fair means or foul.

Harvey Barlow

Eater of many biscuits. Often mistaken for a Year 6.

Joanna Nadin

THE WORST CLASS IN THE WORLD GOES WILD!

Illustrated by Rikin Parekh

BLOOMSBURY CHILDREN'S BOOKS

LONDON OXFORD NEW YORK NEW DELHI SYDNEY

BLOOMSBURY CHILDREN'S BOOKS
Bloomsbury Publishing Plc
50 Bedford Square, London WC1B 3DP, UK
29 Earlsfort Terrace, Dublin 2, Ireland

BLOOMSBURY, BLOOMSBURY CHILDREN'S BOOKS and the Diana logo
are trademarks of Bloomsbury Publishing Plc

First published in Great Britain in 2022 by Bloomsbury Publishing Plc

A catalogue record for this book is available from the British Library

ISBN: PB: 978-1-5266-3353-8; eBook: 978-1-5266-3355-2

2 4 6 8 10 9 7 5 3 1

Printed and bound in Great Britain by CPI Group (UK) Ltd, Croydon CR0 4YY

To find out more about our authors and books visit www.bloomsbury.com
and sign up for our newsletters

For the real Bradley Hunt

– J.N.

For all the AMAZINGLY hard-working folk
at Bloomsbury Children's Books: the editors,
designers, Marketing, Production, and the wonderful
warehouse staff. Thank you so much. x

– R.P.

Our class is the **WORST CLASS IN THE WORLD**.

I know it is the **WORST CLASS IN THE WORLD** because Mrs Bottomley-Blunt (who is our headmistress, and who makes a noise like a horse when she is annoyed, which is a lot) is always taking our teacher into the corridor and saying,

'Mr Nidgett, I have come across some rotten eggs in my time, but 4B is **LITERALLY** the **WORST CLASS IN THE WORLD**.'

LITERALLY means actually scientifically **TRUE**. Mrs Bottomley-Blunt pointed that out when Manjit Morris (who is my best friend, and who is going to be the First Human Boy to Tunnel to the Centre of the Earth) said his head had **LITERALLY** exploded when he got a dog called Killer for his birthday, and it actually hadn't.

It is true that a lot of things do not go as well as they could in class 4B. For example:

1. The time Keith Mears drank Newt Pond Water for a dare and was sick on Mr Nidgett's Emergency Shoes.

2. The time Manjit tried to pull my tooth out with a piece of rope.

3. The time we got a substitute teacher and he let Harvey do an experiment and it exploded foam over everyone.

Plus no one has won a prize all year, and 4A have won:

1. Best Song about Florence Nightingale

2. Best Kennel Made from Recycled Yogurt Pots

3. Best Massive Hat

Although this is not surprising, as their class captain is Eustace Troy, who is president of chess club, first violin in the school orchestra and team leader on the Shining Examples competitive spelling squad.

Our class captain is Bruce Bingley, who can only burp the national anthem, which I think is quite impressive, but Mrs Bottomley-Blunt does not.

BURP!!

She says school is not about footling or fiddle-faddling or **FUN**. It is about **LEARNING** and it is high time we tried harder to **EXCEL** at it.

Dad says well at least I haven't been arrested. Grandpa says being arrested would be getting off lightly and **IN HIS DAY** he had to walk five miles to school barefoot and eat gravel for lunch.

Mum, who works at the council, says, 'I have spent all day listening to Mr Butterworth bang on about bollards and the last thing I need is a heated debate about eating gravel. As long as Stanley's happy, that's all that matters.'

And you know what? I am happy, because:

1. According to Mr Nidgett, everyone excels at something, even Harvey Barlow – they just have to look very hard to find it.

2. According to the laws of probability, we have had all our bad luck and nothing else can possibly go wrong.

3. According to Manjit, even if it does

go wrong we have a FOOLPROOF PLAN
to get away with it, which is DO NOT
TELL ANYONE.

You see, 4B may be the **WORST
CLASS IN THE WORLD**. But I
like it.

The Epic Swaps

Penelope Potts says it's Keith
Mears's fault for trying to swap
his little brother Kevin for a bag of
crisps.

Keith Mears says it's Manjit
Morris's fault for starting Swaps

so he could get the War of the Wizards Wizard Wangle card off Bradley Hunt.

Manjit Morris says it's his box of Krispy Choco Pops's fault for not having the War of the Wizards Wizard Wangle card inside it in the first place.

Mr Nidgett says he doesn't actually care whose fault it is, as long as the Swaps Madness is finished or he will **LITERALLY** resign

14

from teaching and invent a time machine out of an alarm clock and some bottle tops because it cannot be harder than this.

I don't know whose fault it is, but I do know it started on Monday.

On Monday Manjit came to school full of **GLOOM** because he had opened his new box of Krispy Choco Pops to see which free War of the Wizards card was inside, and it was **NOT** the Wizard Wangle card (which is the only one he is missing before he has all one hundred, which would mean he gets a free badge and to meet the Head Wizard, which would be **EPIC**). It was a Boggit card, and he already has eleven of them.

So he was **LITERALLY** going
to explode with sadness as there
was no way he could get a Wizard
Wangle card now because:

1. Mrs Morris has banned Mr
Morris from buying any more
Krispy Choco Pops and it is
Toast Only for breakfast from now on.

2. The only other place to get one is
on the internet for probably nearly a
billion pounds.

3. He doesn't have nearly a billion
pounds, he has four pounds twenty-
three pence and a bent euro.

Which is when I had my
BRILLIANT idea, which was

that maybe he could

SWAP the Boggit

card for a Wizard

Wangle card so

that he has all one

hundred cards. And

Manjit agreed, and said

then he could meet the Head

Wizard **AND** get a free badge **AND**

sell the Wizard Wangle card on the

internet afterwards so he would

also become the First Human Boy

to Be Nearly a **BILLIONAIRE**, which would be **DOUBLY EPIC** and that the plan was **FOOLPROOF** and we would do it at first break.

Only at first break it turned out that no one had a Wizard Wangle card to swap.

Lacey Braithwaite had ten Boggits.

Keith Mears had fourteen Boggits and a Magic Monkey.

Harvey Barlow had twenty Boggits, a Magic Monkey and half a packet of Double Jammo Sandwich Biscuits, which we ate for **BRAIN FOOD** so we could think of where else to get a Wizard Wangle card, but it didn't work.

Which is when Penelope Potts showed up and asked why we were **LURKING** near the Smelly Death Log (which Bruce Bingley claims has an ancient curse, and if anyone touches it for more than a second they will get swallowed by the Ghost Pigeon) because **NO LURKING** is number 104 in Mrs Bottomley-Blunt's list of

rules and she would report us right
NOW unless we confessed what we
were up to.

So Manjit said, 'I will never
confess. Not even if you torture me
with bees or oxtail soup.' Because
oxtail soup is his worst soup.

And I said, 'And anyway,
we weren't **LURKING**, we were
THINKING, which isn't against Mrs
Bottomley-Blunt's rules, not one bit.'

And Penelope said, 'Is.'

And I said, 'Isn't.'

And Penelope said, 'Is.'

And I said, 'Isn't.'

And Penelope said, 'Well, tell me what you're **THINKING** about and then I might not report you.'

So Manjit said, 'We're **THINKING** about who has a Wizard Wangle card so I can swap it and meet the Head Wizard and get a free badge and become the First Human Boy to Be Nearly a **BILLIONAIRE**, which would be **EPIC**.'

And Penelope said why don't we ask Bradley Hunt, who is in a gang with other Bigger Boys, and who has a lot of very **EPIC** things, e.g. a skateboard, hair that **DEFIES GRAVITY**, and a dad who once won a race against an ostrich, while Mr Morris is mainly in his armchair being an **UNDISCOVERED GENIUS** and has never won anything.

And Manjit said this plan was **FOOLPROOF** and in fact Penelope was an **UNDISCOVERED GENIUS** and when he got his nearly a billion pounds, he would give her one of them. And she said in that case she

24

wouldn't report us. And everyone
was happy and the plan was
FOOLPROOF again and we would
do it at lunch.

Only when we went to see Bradley
Hunt at lunch he said in fact he
DID have a Wizard Wangle card
but that he did not want to swap
it for a Boggit card, or a Magic
Monkey card, or even a Weird
Priestess card.

Manjit said, 'So what **WILL** you
swap it for?'

Bradley Hunt said, 'ONE THOUSAND POUNDS, or something really EPIC.' And then he and the rest of the Bigger Boys walked off to do Bigger Boy things.

Only we didn't have ONE THOUSAND POUNDS or anything really EPIC, so Manjit said he was definitely going to LITERALLY explode with sadness now. Only I said perhaps we could FIND something that was epic enough to be SWAPPABLE with Bradley Hunt. Manjit said in fact I was an

UNDISCOVERED GENIUS and that
I could have two of his nearly a
billion pounds and the plan was
FOOLPROOF again and we would
do it after school.

After school we went to Manjit's house to find something **SWAPPABLE**.

Manjit's house is **OUTSTANDING** because Mr Morris is in charge of cleaning and tidying, and he is mainly too busy on the sofa reading the paper, so the house is not very clean or tidy but is full of possibly **SWAPPABLE** things, e.g.:

1. A packet of biscuits that is five years past its use-by date because the biscuits have raisins in them and no one likes raisins unless they are WEIRD.

2. A War of the Wizards Hat of Invincibility that is too small so mostly Killer wears it when Manjit is making her be a Wolf Wizard, which is why it is also a bit chewed.

3. Four dead wasps in a jar.

We decided the most **SWAPPABLE** thing was the four dead wasps in a jar because we could say they were a rare Endangered Wasp which was quite **EPIC**. But Manjit said it still wasn't **EPIC** enough for Bradley Hunt and so he would **LITERALLY** explode with sadness, probably after tea.

Which is when I had my next brilliant idea which was this: what if we swapped our four dead wasps in a jar with someone else who had an even more **EPIC SWAPPABLE** thing?

And then if that **SWAPPABLE** thing wasn't **EPIC** enough, then we could swap it with someone else's even **MORE EPIC SWAPPABLE** thing and we could keep on doing it until we got the **MOST EPIC SWAP EVER**. Then he would be able to get the Wizard Wangle card **AND** the free badge **AND** meet the Head Wizard **AND** become the First Human Boy to Be Nearly a **BILLIONAIRE**. And Manjit said this was definitely a brilliant idea and so the plan had been **FOOLPROOF** all along and he wouldn't explode until at least tomorrow.

So the next day Manjit brought the four dead wasps in a jar to school and said, 'SWAPS at first break behind the Poo Wagon (which is not actually a wagon made of poo, it is the temporary boys' toilets, because Manjit broke the real ones, but that's another story), pass it on!'

So I passed it on to Bruce
Bingley.

And Bruce Bingley passed it on
to Keith Mears.

And Keith Mears passed it on to
Harvey Barlow.

And Harvey Barlow passed it on
to Muriel Lemon.

And Muriel Lemon passed it on to Lacey Braithwaite.

And Lacey Braithwaite passed it on to Lionel Dawes.

And Lionel Dawes passed it on to Penelope Potts, until the whole of 4B knew about the Poo Wagon **SWAPS**.

By first break everyone was **MAD** with excitement about **SWAPS** and had got out their most **SWAPPABLE** thing of all, e.g. Harvey Barlow had got a Chocowham! bar with only one bite taken out of it. Lionel Dawes (who is called Lionel, even though she is a girl, because her mum says names do not have genders, they are just words, which is true if you think about it, but Mrs Bottomley-Blunt does not agree) had got a badge with a unicorn on it.

Keith Mears had got a blue pencil that was a magic blue pencil because every time he used it he got four out of ten in maths instead of only e.g. three or none.

And almost immediately everyone was arguing about who would go first. Keith said it should be him because his pencil was magic, and Harvey said it should be him because otherwise he might have to eat some more Chocowham! bar and there would be less to **SWAP**, and Manjit said it should be him because he had invented **SWAPS** in the first place. And Penelope Potts said he had not.

And Manjit said, 'Have.'

And Penelope said, 'Have not.'

And Manjit said, 'Have.'

So Penelope said, 'Have not and if you say you have one more time I will report you to Mrs Bottomley-Blunt for claiming to have invented something you haven't.' Which is against rule 135.

So Manjit did not say he had invented it any more and Lionel said in fact she would **PUT IT TO THE PEOPLE** about who should go first,

which means have a vote, because
she is very keen on votes, and the
PEOPLE said Manjit could go first.
Which he did and he swapped
the jar of four dead wasps with
Lionel's unicorn badge because he
said they were Endangered and
she is quite keen on Endangered
Wasps and she was going to
revive them later with music and
hummus.

Then Manjit swapped the
unicorn badge for Harvey's
Chocowham! bar with only

one bite taken out. And then he

swapped the Chocowham! bar for

Keith Mears's magic blue pencil.

And then he swapped the magic

blue pencil for Muriel Lemon's

forehead thermometer which

is only four degrees incorrect.

And then he swapped the

forehead thermometer for Lacey

Braithwaite's Real Gold Plastic

Pendant that was once owned by a

pop star.

And then we decided that that

was the **MOST EPIC SWAP** of all

so we took the Real Gold Plastic
Pendant that was once owned by a
pop star to Bradley Hunt, who was
LURKING by the Smelly
Death Log eating
Cheesy Frizzles,
and asked if he
would **SWAP** it
for the Wizard
Wangle card.
But he said
no because it wasn't
EPIC enough.
When we got back to the Poo

Wagon, Manjit said he was definitely **LITERALLY** going to explode with sadness now because he would never meet the Head Wizard **OR** get a free badge **OR** be the First Human Boy to Be Nearly a **BILLIONAIRE**. Only I said what if everyone brought in **EPIC** swaps tomorrow. And everyone said they would. And Manjit said he wouldn't explode just yet then.

And the next day at the Poo Wagon everyone **HAD** brought **EPIC** swaps.

Bruce Bingley had brought a conker that had **NEVER LOST YET** so it was a **BIONIC CONKER**.

Penelope Potts had brought a book about the Queen with one page completely missing.

Harvey Barlow had brought a packet of crisps that was still mostly full.

Keith Mears had brought his little brother Kevin, who can do his twelve times table without even getting one wrong and he is only Year 1 so he is a **PHENOMENON** and anyone who gets him will **ABSORB** the **GENIUS**.

So Lionel **PUT IT TO THE PEOPLE** who should go first and the **PEOPLE** said Keith should go first, so Manjit said the **PEOPLE** were wrong and Lionel said the **PEOPLE** are never wrong and the **PEOPLE** agreed and so Keith went first.

Keith swapped Kevin for Harvey Barlow's packet of crisps that was still mostly full. And then he swapped the packet of crisps with

Bruce Bingley's **BIONIC CONKER**. And then he swapped the **BIONIC CONKER** for Manjit's packet of biscuits that is five years past its use-by date because the biscuits have raisins in them and no one likes raisins unless they are **WEIRD**, because he is **WEIRD** and he doesn't care who says it.

And Manjit was happy because he said that was the **MOST EPIC SWAP** of all so we took the **BIONIC CONKER** to Bradley Hunt, who was **LURKING** by the Smelly Death Log

eating Cheesy Frizzles again, and
asked if he would **SWAP** it for the
Wizard Wangle card.

But he said no because
it wasn't **EPIC** enough.

When we got back to the Poo Wagon, Manjit said he was **LITERALLY** going to explode with sadness any minute. But I said what if we went to Paradise City after school and got a packet of Cheesy Frizzles because Bradley Hunt definitely thinks they are **EPIC** because he is always eating them. And Manjit said that was definitely **FOOLPROOF** and so he wouldn't explode just yet and we would take Killer because she always needed a poo around then

and she especially liked to poo
near Paradise City.

Paradise City is a shop on the
corner and has a sign that says:

We Sell
Everything

only it doesn't sell:

1. Night-vision swimming goggles.

2. Antique ski poles.

3. A stuffed monkey holding an orange.

4. Live snakes.

5. Dead dinosaur eggs.

6. A piece of moon in a box.

7. A plum with a maggot in.

8. A gold-plated toilet brush.

9. A scale model of a
combustion engine.

10. The Emperor of Zarg

Because Manjit has tested it. But
it **DOES** sell Cheesy Frizzles. Only
when we got there, Mrs Beasley
(who is in charge, and whose
eyebrows meet in the middle,
which Manjit says means she is a
werewolf) said she had just sold
the last packet of Cheesy Frizzles

and it so it was Bacon Bangers or nothing.

Manjit said, 'What if I swapped you a **BIONIC CONKER**?'

But Mrs Beasley said she didn't want a **BIONIC CONKER** and if we didn't stop **FOOLING ABOUT** and also get that **BLESSED DOG** out of here then we would be **BARRED FOR LIFE**.

And Manjit said, 'But not **LITERALLY** life.'

And she said, 'Yes, **LITERALLY** until you are dead.'

And so we stopped and got the **BLESSED DOG** out. And Manjit said he was going to **LITERALLY** explode **RIGHT NOW** and so I should stand back and count to ten and I did stand back but before I could get to three a voice said '**EPIC** dog' and the voice was Bradley Hunt! Which I said was a **COINCIDENCE**, which means something spooky accidentally happening at the same time, and Manjit said it was because of the **BIONIC CONKER**.

Manjit said, 'She is actually the

MOST EPIC dog ever and you can **SWAP** her if you like for the Wizard Wangle card.'

Which is when Bradley said, 'OK then, hand her over and I will bring the card to school tomorrow. Meet me at the Poo Wagon at first break.'

And so Manjit did hand Killer
over and off went Bradley Hunt
with his new dog. I said wouldn't
Manjit's mum and dad mind about
Killer, but Manjit said no because
Killer had eaten Mrs Morris's best
pants yesterday and they were still
arguing about whose fault it was.
Plus now he was going to meet the

Head Wizard
AND get
a free
badge
AND be

the First Human Boy to Be Nearly a **BILLIONAIRE** so in fact they would be happy, and I agreed.

And Manjit was right because when we got back to his house Mr Morris didn't even notice that Killer was missing and Mrs Morris was busy being a policewoman at night so she would be **NONE THE WISER**.

The next day Manjit was **MAD** with excitement about getting the Wizard Wangle card at first break.

And everyone else was **MAD** with excitement as well because there was someone else in class and that was Kevin Mears.

Mr Nidgett said, 'Can someone please tell me why Kevin Mears is in here?'

Penelope Potts said, 'Because Keith Mears swapped him with Harvey Barlow for a packet of crisps and then I swapped him with Harvey for a book about the Queen with a page completely missing because he is a **PHENOMENON** and so I will **ABSORB** the **GENIUS**.' Because she wants to move to 4A because her sister Hermione is already there and it is **UNFAIR**.

And I could tell Mr Nidgett was about to say something about that when in walked someone else who shouldn't have been in class and that was Bradley Hunt, and Killer!

Mr Nidgett said, 'Can someone please tell me why Bradley Hunt and Killer are in here and also why Bradley is wearing jogging bottoms?'

Bradley said, 'Because I **SWAPPED** Killer with Manjit because I thought she was **EPIC** but she is not.'

And it turns out that Killer did a lot of **NON-EPIC** things at Bradley Hunt's house, e.g.:

1. Ate Bradley's school trousers.

2. Ate Mrs Hunt's third-best shoes.

3. Did a poo in the airing cupboard

(because Killer is keen on airing cupboards and she had not had time for her poo at Paradise City).

And so he wanted to cancel the **SWAP**, i.e. give Killer back and keep the Wizard Wangle card after all.

Only Manjit said no way, because how else was he going to meet the Head Wizard **AND** get a free badge **AND** be the First Human Boy to Be Nearly a **BILLIONAIRE** unless Bradley swapped it for something else **EPIC**? And Keith Mears said he could swap the Wizard Wangle card for Kevin, and then Keith could swap the card with Manjit for a fair share of the **BILLION** pounds, e.g. twenty-five. Only Penelope Potts said no he could not because now **SHE** owned Kevin so in fact **SHE** should get the twenty-five pounds.

And Keith said, 'Do not!'

And Penelope said, 'Do!'

And Keith said, 'Do not!'

And Penelope said, 'Do!'

Which is when Bradley said there was no way he could swap the Wizard Wangle card for anything, not even if it was the most **EPIC** thing ever, and definitely not Kevin, because in fact as well as the trousers and shoes and the poo in the cupboard, Killer had eaten the card.

Manjit said he was **LITERALLY**

going to explode with sadness right there and then and we should start counting. But Bruce Bingley said actually we just needed to hold Killer upside down until she was sick, because before he had stuck the plastic brontosaurus up his nose, he had actually swallowed it, but Mrs Bingley held him upside down and it had come right out again.

So Manjit tried to hold Killer upside down but Killer did not like being held upside down, and howled, so he let go and she went under the

desk and did a protest wee, which
went on to my shoes, so I had to put
on Mr Nidgett's emergency ones,
which were too big, and so I tripped
over and fell on the floor.

Which is when Mrs Bottomley-
Blunt walked in. She said, 'Mr
Nidgett, WHY on earth is there wee
on the floor and a dog under the
desk, and why are Bradley Hunt
and Kevin Mears in here, and why is
Stanley Bradshaw wearing TOO-BIG
shoes and lying on the floor, which
is breaking two rules at once?'

Mr Nidgett said it was a long story, involving **SWAPS**, and Mrs Bottomley-Blunt said in that case she was confiscating everyone's **SWAPS** until the end of the day, including Kevin Mears and Killer. And making a new rule against **SWAPS**. And putting us all on the Disappointing Day board. 'Mr Nidgett,' she carried on. 'I have met some rotten eggs in my time, but 4B is **LITERALLY** the **WORST CLASS IN THE WORLD**.' And then she stormed out with Bradley

Hunt, and Kevin, and Killer, and the swallowed-up Wizard Wangle card.

Which is when everyone started arguing about whose fault it was and Mr Nidgett said he didn't actually care whose fault it was, as long as the Swaps Madness was finished, or he would **LITERALLY** resign from teaching and invent a time machine out of an alarm clock and some bottle tops because it could not be harder than this.

When I got home, Grandpa said, 'Why are you wearing **TOO-BIG** shoes? Have you been up to no good with That Manjit again?'

I said I hadn't, we had only swapped Killer for a Wizard Wangle card with someone from the Bigger Boys gang and it had gone a bit wrong.

Dad said, 'I was in a gang. We did Interpretive Dance.'

Grandpa said, '**IN MY DAY** we couldn't afford to be in **GANGS**, we just fought with broom handles.'

And Mum said, 'I've just spent all day listening to Mr Butterworth bang on about radiators so the last thing I need is a heated debate about broom handles. As long as Stanley's happy, that's all that matters.'

And do you know what? I am. Because even though Killer

swallowed the Wizard Wangle card, it turned out that the Krispy Choco Pops offer closed about a month ago and no one got all one hundred cards so no one gets the free badge **OR** to meet the Head Wizard, but Manjit still might be the First Human Boy to Be Nearly a **BILLIONAIRE**.

We just have to think of some more **FOOLPROOF PLANS**.

The Best Teacher in the World

Lacey Braithwaite says it's Keith
Mears's fault for saying Harvey
Barlow was King Harold's horse
and throwing **REALISTIC** blood all
over Harvey's head.

Keith Mears says it's Harvey

Barlow's fault for saying Keith Mears was King Harold and throwing **REALISTIC** blood all over Keith Mears's head.

Manjit Morris says it's Mr Winterbottom's fault for letting us use **REALISTIC** blood for the Battle of Hastings in the first place.

Mr Winterbottom says he doesn't actually care whose fault it is, as long as Mr Nidgett comes back tomorrow because he is going to **LITERALLY** resign from supply teaching and set up his own **SCHOOL OF IMAGINATION** where he can teach what he likes and no one will wear shoes ever.

I don't know whose fault it is, but I do know it started on Thursday.

What happened was, Thursday morning had been completely **NORMAL**, e.g.:

1. Lacey Braithwaite claimed she could play 'If I Had a Hammer' on the recorder without even getting a note

79

wrong, and she could not.

2. Bruce Bingley claimed he could VANQUISH Lacey Braithwaite and her recorder with the POWER OF HIS EYES by staring at her without blinking for a whole minute, and he could not.

3. Keith Mears claimed he could VANQUISH Bruce Bingley with the POWER OF HIS EYES by staring at him for a whole HOUR without blinking, and he could not.

And Mr Nidgett said, 'Perhaps it's time to stop playing recorders and staring and start working out if you can use a semicolon in the right place in a sentence.' And not one of us could, not even Penelope Potts. But he didn't put us on the Disappointing Day board because he said at least we had tried and it is the trying that counts. Plus it is already full from the time we came to school dressed as **MOOGOLs**, but that's another story.

Thursday afternoon had been

completely **NORMAL**, i.e. we played Would You Rather.

Manjit said, 'Would you rather drink Newt Pond Water with poo in it or bin juice?'

I said is the bin juice hot or cold and he said hot so I said Newt Pond Water with poo in it.

So Manjit said, 'Would you rather drink bin juice, or lick sick?'

I said is the sick human sick or e.g. goose sick and he said human sick so I said drink bin juice.

So Manjit said, 'Would you rather lick sick or touch a ghost who would explode you?'

I said would the ghost definitely explode me or only maybe explode me and Manjit said only maybe so I said the ghost.

And that is when Mr Nidgett said, 'Perhaps it's time to stop discussing sick and bin juice and start working out if you can spell

"**DEFINITELY**" without getting it wrong.' And not one of us could, not even Penelope Potts. But he didn't put us on the Disappointing Day board because he said at least we had tried and it is the trying that counts. Plus it is still already full.

But when we came back to class after last break, it was not **NORMAL** because Mr Nidgett had vanished into **THIN AIR** and instead Mrs Bottomley-Blunt was there making a noise like a horse

and saying that Mr Nidgett had
had an emergency.

And then we were all arguing
about what sort of an emergency
Mr Nidgett was having and why he
hadn't taken his Emergency Shoes
with him.

Penelope
Potts said he had
probably been
summoned by the
government to be awarded a
top prize for being the **BEST
TEACHER IN THE WORLD**

and so he
would have to
wear new shoes
with sparkle on
them.

Manjit said he had
probably been
summoned by
the government
to become a **SPY**
and so he would
have special shoes
with radar in them
and also a laser

eyeball that he could take out
when he needed it.

Keith Mears said he had
probably been summoned by
the government to become an
OVERLORD OF THE UNIVERSE
and they don't

even wear

shoes because

their feet

are made of

STEEL.

But Mrs Bottomley-Blunt said:

1. It was NONE OF OUR BUSINESS what the emergency was but that it was definitely NOT any of these things.

2. Mr Nidgett was not the BEST TEACHER IN THE WORLD otherwise we wouldn't think OVERLORDS OF THE UNIVERSE were real (they are).

3. Mr Nidgett would not be back for at least a day so we would be getting a supply teacher and an actual one this time, not Mrs Pickens (who is our school secretary and who smells of soup), and the less said about THAT the better.

And immediately everyone was arguing again about who the supply teacher might be.

Harvey Barlow said it might be the man who invented Double Jammo Sandwich Biscuits, who he wished was his dad, because then he'd get a free supply forever.

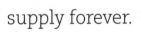

Lacey Braithwaite said it might be **HER** dad, who had invented noodle strudel, only no one else agreed it was genius yet, not even her mum.

Bruce Bingley said it might be the Emperor of Zarg, who was actually **HIS** dad and he wasn't even lying this time.

And Penelope said, 'Are.'

And Bruce said, 'Am not.'

And Penelope said, 'Are.'

And Bruce said, 'Not.'

But Mrs Bottomley-Blunt said that was **QUITE ENOUGH** and it would not be any of these people as none of them was qualified to work with children, especially not the Emperor of Zarg, who wasn't even real, but that whoever it was we were to be on our **BEST BEHAVIOUR**.

And I could tell Bruce Bingley was about to argue but then he did not because 'No arguing with Mrs Bottomley-Blunt **EVER**' is rule 150. Then Mrs Bottomley-Blunt said she would read us a story about a goat for the rest of the afternoon and we were to start being on our

BEST BEHAVIOUR right now and we almost were.

The next day when we came into class, there was our supply teacher and it wasn't the man who had invented Double Jammo Sandwich Biscuits, or Lacey Braithwaite's dad, or the Emperor of Zarg. It was another man, with very, very shaggy hair, and he was called Mr Winterbottom, and we knew this because he'd written on the whiteboard in rainbow-coloured

92

pens and it said 'Welcome, Class 4B. My name is Mr Winterbottom!' and underneath he'd drawn a picture of something that looked like a unicorn wearing a helmet of frogs.

Lionel Dawes put her hand up (which is part of **BEST BEHAVIOUR**) and said, 'Is that a picture of a giraffe going to a wedding?'

Mr Winterbottom said, 'Thank you for

your question which is full of
IMAGINATION. And the answer
is it can be whatever you want
it to be because art is in the
EYE OF THE BEHOLDER.' Which
means it is up to you and whether
something is good or not.

So Keith Mears said in fact it
was a picture of the Emperor of
Zarg eating his nemesis, the King
of Zog, after turning him into **POO**.

But Bruce Bingley said it was
the King of Zog eating the Emperor
of Zarg but he didn't need to turn

him into **POO** because he already
WAS POO.

Only then Manjit said it
was him eating the Emperor of
Zarg and the King of Zog, only
they weren't **POO**, they were the
Strongest Cheese in the World,
and he would not be sick, not even
once (because he is quite keen
on becoming the First Human
Boy to Eat an Entire Wheel of the

Strongest Cheese in the World without Being Sick).

And Mr Winterbottom said we all had excellent **IMAGINATIONS** and that would be good for our first lesson.

So we all got out our literacy books because it was Friday. Only Mr Winterbottom said, 'Hold your horses, gang!' (which means 'Stop what you're doing right now') and to put the books away because literacy was all about commas and capital letters and colons, which are **RULES**, and he did not believe in **RULES** only **IMAGINATIONS**.

Lionel Dawes said in fact Mr
Winterbottom was the **BEST
TEACHER IN THE WORLD**
(because her mum does not believe
in rules either, which is why Lionel

sometimes
comes to
school in a
cat outfit and
has to be sent
home) because
not even Mr
Nidgett let us
off literacy.

Then he was definitely the

BEST TEACHER IN THE WORLD

because he said in fact it would

be up to us to decide what we did

today.

Lionel said maybe we could

hunt for the Endangered Wasp,

because she is very keen on saving

an Endangered Wasp, and also

whales.

Bruce Bingley said maybe we

could hunt for the Ghost Pigeon,

which will swallow you if you

touch the poo on the Smelly Death

Log for even a second, because of
the curse.

Manjit said maybe we could
hunt for a YETI, because then he
would be the First Human Boy to
Find a Yeti and Befriend It.

And Mr Winterbottom said
these were all brilliant ideas full
of IMAGINATION, but how about
we went on a NATURE WALK and
even if we did not find a wasp or
a ghost pigeon or a yeti, we would
find something INTERESTING.

I said, but we hadn't brought

our wellies, and we are not supposed to do nature walks in our school shoes, not after last time. So Mr Winterbottom said we would do it with **BARE FEET** because that way we could **FEEL** nature as well as see it and Lionel Dawes agreed.

Only Muriel Lemon (whose parents are both doctors, and who is excused from all dangerous activities, e.g. netball, football and science experiments) said, 'What about thistles and poo?'

Mr Winterbottom said he would keep a special eye out for them and anyway it would only be in the playground as Mrs Bottomley-Blunt said he wasn't allowed to leave the premises, not until **KINGDOM COME** but he was hoping it would come soon. And I said we were all waiting for that but it hadn't come yet.

So then we were all **MAD** with excitement and took off our shoes (except Muriel Lemon) and trooped out to the playground with a see-through plastic box from Mr Winterbottom's **TEACHING BAG OF WONDER** to put our **NATURE** treasure in and these are the things we found:

1. An acorn, which we didn't put in the plastic box because Keith Mears threw it at Harvey Barlow and it got lost.

2. A spider with only seven legs, which we didn't put in the plastic box because it was busy making a web to catch flies and we agreed flies were EVIL.

3. Four newts in the newt pond, which we didn't put in the plastic box because it is against the List of Rules, and so is borrowing them so they can be our dragon minions.

4. Lionel Dawes's cat, Dave (who is called Dave even though it is a girl, and

who is not allowed on school property
because it is against the rules but
Dave doesn't understand rules), which
we tried to put in the plastic box but
Dave wasn't keen on this and
went for a poo in Mr
Spigot's vegetable
bed instead.
5. The dead pigeon
near the slide that has been there
for a week and no one has moved
it because Manjit says it is going
to be the New Ghost Pigeon and will
LITERALLY chew anyone who touches it.

Which Penelope Potts said

definitely wasn't true.

And Manjit said, 'Is.'

And Penelope said, 'Isn't.'

And Manjit said, 'Is.'

And Penelope said, 'Isn't.'

But Mr Winterbottom said

it didn't matter if it was true

or not because it was full of

IMAGINATION, but it was a shame

if it was true because then we

couldn't put the dead pigeon

into a plastic box and watch it

turn into a skeleton which is

NATURE IN ACTION and also **SCIENCE**. So Manjit said it might not be **LITERALLY** true and so Mr Winterbottom put the pigeon in the box after all. And we were just about to troop back to the classroom when Mrs Bottomley-Blunt appeared and said, 'What do you think you're doing outside with no shoes on and a dead pigeon in a box?'

Mr Winterbottom said we were having a **NATURE WALK** and also doing science but Mrs Bottomley-Blunt said, 'That is not how science is taught at this school. Science is **INSIDE** with **SHOES ON**.' And then she sent for Mr Spigot (who is our caretaker, and has one ear bigger than the other) to put the dead pigeon in the bin and made us troop back inside to put our shoes on, which Manjit said was a shame because now Mr Spigot might get chewed by the **NEW GHOST PIGEON**, and Mr Winterbottom said was a shame because now we could not **FEEL** nature, but Mrs Bottomley-Blunt said it was not a shame, it was **SENSIBLE**, and Mr Winterbottom would never be a good teacher if he wasn't **SENSIBLE**.

On the way back Mr Winterbottom did **FEEL** nature because he trod on a wasp, which Lionel Dawes said was sad for the wasp, and Muriel Lemon said was **INEVITABLE**, and Mr Winterbottom said was just **NATURE IN ACTION** (even though he had to put on Mr Nidgett's Emergency Shoes because his foot swelled up and went red), but that he could still do science and it was up to us what science we did.

So immediately everyone was arguing about what science we should do.

Lacey Braithwaite said we should **MELT** things and we could start with the plastic nature box.

Keith Mears said we should **EXPLODE** things and we could start with Mr Winterbottom's disused shoes.

Manjit said we should **MELT AND EXPLODE** things and we could start with Mrs Bottomley-Blunt.

Mr Winterbottom said all those answers were full of **IMAGINATION** but that we could start with an experiment with a minty sweet and a big bottle of fizzy drink to show how **CHEMISTRY** worked and there would be an **EXPLOSION** but only a small one and the fizzy pop would foam over the top of the bottle and into the plastic box.

And so he got his **TEACHING BAG OF WONDER** and took out a minty sweet and the bottle of fizzy pop, which Penelope Potts said was against Mrs Bottomley-Blunt's List of Rules, but Mr Winterbottom said was in the **NAME OF SCIENCE** so she wouldn't mind. So

Harvey Barlow got out his own minty sweets in the **NAME OF SCIENCE** and we all had one, but there were still thirteen left over, and so Harvey said we should add them to the experiment in the **NAME OF SCIENCE**.

And that is where it all went wrong.

Because the explosion wasn't small; it was quite large and loud and whooshy. And the fizzy pop didn't just foam down the bottle and into the box, it foamed …

All over Harvey Barlow.

And all over Keith Mears.

And all over Bruce Bingley.

And all over Penelope Potts.

And all over Lacey Braithwaite.

And all over Lionel Dawes.

And all over Muriel Lemon, even though she is excused from science.

And all over Manjit.

And all over me.

And all over Mr Winterbottom, who had to take off Mr Nidgett's Emergency Shoes.

Which is when Mrs Bottomley-
Blunt walked in and asked why
was Mr Winterbottom barefoot
again when he knew very well that
science was taught with **SHOES ON**.
And why were we all soggy. And
why was there an empty bottle of
fizzy pop on the table when fizzy
pop was against the rules.

Mr Winterbottom said it was all
in the **NAME OF SCIENCE** and that
you couldn't make an omelette
without breaking eggs. But Mrs
Bottomley-Blunt said making

omelettes at school was definitely against the rules and from now on we had to do something **SAFE** like **HISTORY**, and we had to do it with **SHOES ON**.

And everyone went, '**OHHHHHH**,' because history isn't as good as **MELTING** or **EXPLODING** things. But Mrs Bottomley-Blunt said any more '**OHHHing**' and we would all be on the Disappointing Day board even though it was full, and then she stomped off to fetch Mr Spigot to mop up.

But when the mopping up was done, Mr Winterbottom said in fact we could choose what bit of **HISTORY** to learn about, e.g. a **WAR**.

So immediately everyone was arguing about which **WAR** to learn.

Muriel Lemon said it should be the Crimean **WAR**.

Keith Mears said it should be **WAR** of the Wizards.

Manjit said it should be **WAR** against Keith Mears.

Mr Winterbottom said all those answers were full of **IMAGINATION**

and that he hoped we knew **WAR**
was **WRONG**. But how about the
BATTLE of Hastings, which was
actually a bit of a **WAR** and King
Harold was in it and he got shot
in the eye with an arrow and that
he had an arrow in his **TEACHING**
BAG OF WONDER and it was
REALISTIC even though it only
had a plastic sucker on the end,
not a point.

And everyone agreed that
getting shot in the eye with an
arrow was **OUTSTANDING** even if

it only had a plastic sucker on it.

And Bruce Bingley said we could use **RED PAINT** so that we had **REALISTIC** blood as well. And Mr Winterbottom agreed and said the shiny floor was the **DESIGNATED BATTLE AREA** and the carpet was the hospital and stables and barracks.

Muriel Lemon said she would use toilet paper as **REALISTIC** bandages to mop up the blood in the hospital.

Harvey Barlow said he would use biscuits as **REALISTIC** rations for the barracks.

Manjit said he would go and fetch **KILLER** as a **REALISTIC** horse for the stable. And Mr Winterbottom said that was full of **IMAGINATION** but maybe one of us could be the horse instead.

And immediately everyone was arguing about who would be the horse and who would be King Harold.

Keith Mears said Harvey Barlow was King Harold's horse and threw **REALISTIC** blood all over Harvey's head.

Harvey Barlow said Keith Mears was King Harold and threw **REALISTIC** blood all over Keith's head.

Lionel Dawes said it was **UNFAIR** to **HORSES** to throw **REALISTIC** blood on them so Manjit threw

REALISTIC blood all over her head.

Penelope Potts said it was
UNFAIR that King Harold was
a man so Bruce Bingley threw
REALISTIC blood all over her head.

Lacey Braithwaite said it was
UNFAIR that she didn't get any
REALISTIC blood so Penelope Potts
threw **REALISTIC** blood all over her
head.

And then everyone threw
REALISTIC blood over everyone
else, including Mr Winterbottom
AND Mrs Bottomley-Blunt, who had

walked into the room right then

and Manjit said she had gone into

the **DESIGNATED BATTLE AREA**

but Mrs Bottomley-Blunt did not

agree.

She said we were **LITERALLY** the **WORST CLASS IN THE WORLD** and Mr Winterbottom was the **WORST TEACHER** and she would be reporting him for it and for not wearing shoes and he would not be coming back to school again, not until **KINGDOM COME**.

Which is when everyone started arguing about whose fault it was and Mr Winterbottom said he was going to **LITERALLY** resign from supply teaching and set up his own **SCHOOL OF IMAGINATION**

where he can teach what he likes

and no one will wear shoes ever.

When I got home, Grandpa said, 'Why are you covered in red paint? Have you been up to no good with That Manjit again?'

I said I hadn't, and it wasn't red paint, it was **REALISTIC BLOOD** from our history lesson.

Dad said, 'We used ketchup instead of paint but only on chips and never in history.'

Grandpa said, '**IN MY DAY** we couldn't afford chips; we ate raw potatoes and were grateful for it.'

Mum said, 'I've just spent all day listening to Mr Butterworth bang on about fences so the last thing I need is a heated debate about raw potatoes. As long as Stanley's happy, that's all that matters.'

And do you know what? I am.

Because Mr Nidgett had not been summoned by anyone, he had just gone to see Mrs Nidgett in hospital because she was having a baby and he said that we could help him name the baby later.

And we did and the baby is called Harold Zarg Nidgett.

And because last week Mr Winterbottom sent us a postcard from his new **SCHOOL OF IMAGINATION** and said we could come on a visit if Mrs Bottomley-Blunt lets us. And she said that would be when **KINGDOM COMES**. Which is usually never.

But then again, you never know what will happen in class 4B, so maybe it will come tomorrow after all.

Mrs Bottomley-Blunt's List of Rules

1. No running in the corridors.

2. No sliding in the corridors.

3. No playing ludo in the corridors.

4. No outside voices inside.

5. No outside voices outside.

6. No putting paper in plugholes to see if it will block them.

7. No putting anything down the toilet.

8. Especially no putting PE kit down the toilet.

9. No eating in class.

10. No eating in the corridors.

11. No eating mud anywhere.

12. No claiming you will eat the class hamster.

13. No claiming you are secretly royal.

14. No claiming you are actually dead.

15. No claiming Major Wellington is a vampire.

16. No hats.

17. No badges.

18. No yo-yos.

19. No fake swords.

20. No real swords.

21. No wearing a colander on
    your head instead of a hat.

22. No being rude.

23. No being greedy.

24. No being too clever by half.

25. No War of the Wizards cards.

26. No War of the Wizards cloaks.

27. No War of the Wizards wands.

28. No ketchup.

Wizard hats are NOT uniform

29. No frogs in jars.

30. No frogspawn in jars

31. No claiming sago pudding is frogspawn.

32. No claiming bubble tea is frogspawn.

33. No claiming anything is frogspawn.

34. No pretending to be deaf.

35. No pretending to be daft.

Shopping

Rubbers
Soap
A loud bell
A mop
Ear plugs

36. No being daft.

37. No hitting each other.

38. No pinching each other.

39. No biting each other.

40. No poking each other.

41. No twisting anyone's ears.

42. No pulling anyone's hair.

43. No fighting in general.

44. No kerfuffle.

45. No shenanigans.

46. No tomfoolery.

47. No showing off.

48. No footling.

49. No fiddle-faddling.

50. No shilly-shallying.

Disappointing Day List

Keith Mears
Harvey Barlow
Bruce Bingley
All of 4B

Mrs Bottomley-Blunt's List of Rules Part 2

51. No eating a whole packet of biscuits.

52. No dropping one biscuit and then eating the rest of the packet.

53. No claiming a Ghost Pigeon ate half the packet.

54. No claiming a Ghost Pigeon ate your homework.

55. No claiming a Ghost Pigeon stole your PE kit.

56. No claiming a Ghost Pigeon spilt the paint.

57. No claiming Ghost Pigeons even exist.

58. No claiming Ghost Monkeys exist.

59. No claiming Ghost Teachers exist.

60. No claiming Major Wellington is a Ghost Teacher.

61. No fizzy drinks.

62. No fizzy sweets.

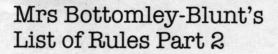

4B Zoo Trip
October 11th
(WARN ZOO)

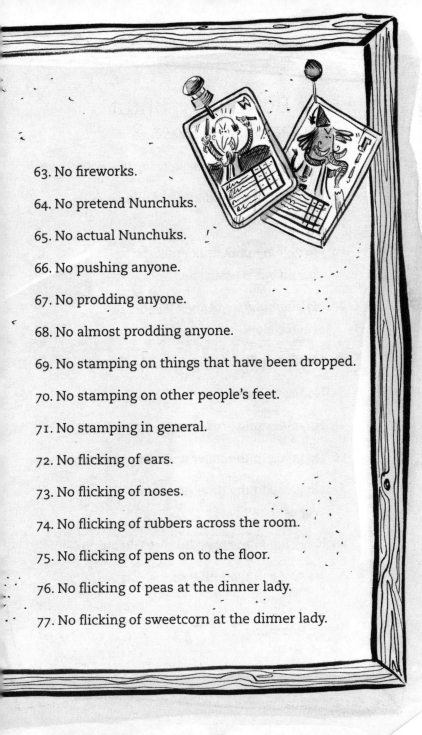

63. No fireworks.

64. No pretend Nunchuks.

65. No actual Nunchuks.

66. No pushing anyone.

67. No prodding anyone.

68. No almost prodding anyone.

69. No stamping on things that have been dropped.

70. No stamping on other people's feet.

71. No stamping in general.

72. No flicking of ears.

73. No flicking of noses.

74. No flicking of rubbers across the room.

75. No flicking of pens on to the floor.

76. No flicking of peas at the dinner lady.

77. No flicking of sweetcorn at the dinner lady.

78. No flicking of anything ever.

79. No spilling soup and claiming it is ectoplasm.

80. No spilling custard and claiming it is ectoplasm.

81. No spilling pink milk and claiming it is ectoplasm.

82. No claiming anything is ectoplasm.

83. No pink milk.

84. No brown milk.

85. No milk except milk milk.

86. No going to the toilet without permission.

87. No going to the toilet to discuss War of the Wizards.

88. No going to the toilet to play Wrestling Club.

89. No going to the toilet unless you actually need the toilet.

90. No Wrestling Club.

91. No War of the Wizards Club.

92. No Vampire Club.

93. No Thinking Up New Clubs Club.

94. No singing the wrong words to hymns.

95. No burping hymns.

96. No burping at all in assembly.

97. No trying to hold your breath for ten minutes in assembly.

98. No trying to make anyone else hold their breath for ten minutes in assembly.

99. No doing anything in assembly except listening and being NEAT and OBEDIENT.

100. No cats.

Mrs Bottomley-Blunt's List of Rules Part 3

101. No causing a HOO-HA.

102. No lying.

103. No pets.

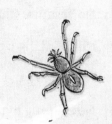

104. No lurking.

105. No having gang meetings.

106. No claiming to be a mouse who has had its cheese stolen so you can be noisy.

107. No annoying Mr Spigot when he's busy.

108. No eating jam sandwiches in class.

109. No eating bananas in class.

110. No bananas in class at all.

111. No coming to school in anything except uniform.

112. No claiming the Ghost Pigeon stole your uniform.

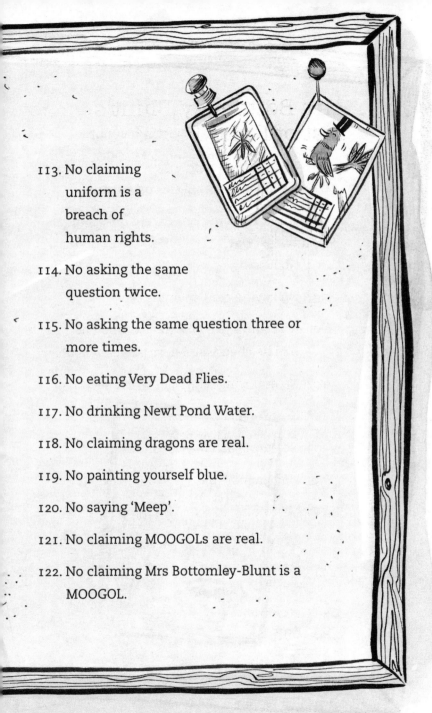

113. No claiming uniform is a breach of human rights.

114. No asking the same question twice.

115. No asking the same question three or more times.

116. No eating Very Dead Flies.

117. No drinking Newt Pond Water.

118. No claiming dragons are real.

119. No painting yourself blue.

120. No saying 'Meep'.

121. No claiming MOOGOLs are real.

122. No claiming Mrs Bottomley-Blunt is a MOOGOL.

123. No arguing with Mrs Bottomley-Blunt when she says she is not a MOOGOL.

124. No deliberately being sick on anyone.

125. No minibeasts in class except on Minibeast Day.

Shopping

Biscuits (plain)
Crackers (plain)
Hairspray (super strong)
Goat feed (plenty)

Mrs Bottomley-Blunt's List of Rules Part 4

Get Mr Spigot to count newts

126. No claiming cats are minibeasts.

127. No claiming dogs are minibeasts.

128. No swaps.

129. No borrowing newts to pretend they are your dragon minions.

130. No going down the slide head first.

131. No going down the slide on your tummy feet first.

132. No lying on the floor.

133. No wearing too-big shoes.

134. No claiming to have invented invisibility helmets.

135. No claiming to have invented anything you haven't.

136. No claiming pigeons are in league with aliens.

137. No claiming Mrs Bottomley-Blunt is in league with aliens.

138. No claiming aliens are real.

139. No claiming you are an alien.

140. No wellingtons in class except in an emergency.

141. No claiming being tired is an emergency.

142. No claiming maths is an emergency.

143. No claiming maths is worse than broccoli.

144. No claiming broccoli is worse than maths.

145. No putting newts in a plastic box.

146. No telling the Year 1s that newts are dragons.

Call
Mr Morris
(again)

147. No telling the Year 1s that eating lemon slices is cool.

148. No telling the Year 1s that wearing wellingtons in class is cool.

149. No telling the Year 1s anything that you have not had permission from Mrs Bottomley-Blunt to tell them.

150. No arguing with Mrs Bottomley-Blunt EVER.

Could
you be in
THE

WORST

CLASS

IN THE

WORLD?

Turn over and take
a fun quiz to find out!

1. Would you swap a trading card for a magic blue pencil?

YES or NO

2. Would you swap your pet for a trading card?

YES or NO

3. Would you swap a sibling (your brother or sister, real or imaginary) for a packet of crisps?

YES or NO

4. Have you ever done a nature walk in the school playground with BARE FEET?

YES or NO

5. Have you ever made a fizzy minty EXPLOSION?

YES or NO

6. Have you ever recreated a battle scene using REALISTIC blood?

YES or NO

ANSWERS

Mostly YES – You could absolutely be one of the Worst Class in the World! Come and join in the fun!

Mostly NO – Sorry, you're probably more suited to being in Class 4A, but you can definitely still play with 4B at breaktime!

Read more hilarious HIGH JINKS with
THE WORST CLASS IN THE WORLD

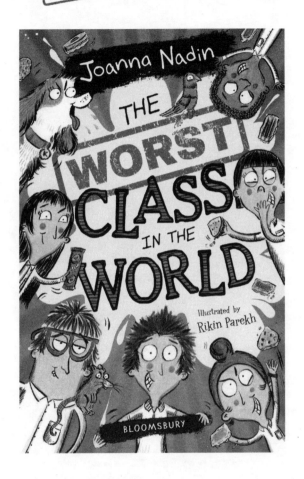

Can you possibly imagine what happens when Stanley and Manjit decide to become Biscuit Kings and win Show and Tell?

TURN OVER FOR A SNEAK PEEK!

Lacey Braithwaite says it's Harvey Barlow's fault for bringing in discount biscuits.

Harvey Barlow says it's Manjit Morris's fault for offering him a broken yo-yo and a stone that might be a dinosaur claw for a discount biscuit.

Manjit says it's Lacey Braithwaite's fault for claiming her biscuits are superior, and also for being so mean with her biscuits in the first place.

Mr Nidgett says he doesn't actually care whose fault it is as long as the Biscuit Madness is finished or he will **LITERALLY** resign from teaching and become a llama farmer because it cannot be harder than this.

I don't know whose fault it is,
but I do know it started on Monday.

What happened was that Manjit
and me were footling around
at first break, up to nothing in
particular, when Manjit saw Lacey
Braithwaite hiding behind the
Smelly Death Log, i.e. the hollow
log with the bird poo on it, which
no one even goes near unless they
are up to **NO GOOD**. Not since Bruce
Bingley claimed it had an ancient

curse on it and if you touched the poo for more than a second you would be swallowed by The Ghost Pigeon.

Manjit said we should spy on Lacey and see what she was up to, because it was bound to be **SUSPICIOUS**. Which it totally was,

because when we got there, we saw that she had got a WHOLE packet of biscuits, which is against:

1. Mr Nidgett's Healthy Snacking guidelines (i.e. one piece of fruit or one nutritious biscuit), and

2. NO BEING GREEDY and NO SHOWING OFF, which are numbers 23 and 47 in Mrs Bottomley-Blunt's List of Rules (the actual List of Rules is laminated and stuck to her door and nothing can remove it, not even a metal ruler, which Manjit has tried) and

3. The curse of the Smelly Death Log.

So I said we should report her
to Mr Nidgett immediately so
he could put her name on the
Disappointing Day board and then
she would lose five minutes of
golden time and have to tidy paint
pots instead.

Only Manjit said actually he
was quite peckish, even though he

had already

eaten his

banana and

also my

banana

(because he is in training to be the First Human Boy to Eat Ten Bananas in Ten Seconds) and that he quite fancied a biscuit, and Lacey would have to give us one each because otherwise we might report her. It was a **FOOLPROOF PLAN** so I agreed.

Only when we asked Lacey Braithwaite, she said, 'No way and anyway these biscuits are too fancy for you, because these are **SUPERIOR** biscuits, because the biscuit bit is made with butter

from the world's most expensive
cows and the jam in the middle is
made with strawberries picked by
highly trained monkeys.'

Manjit said that was a lie, and
Lacey said, 'Is not.'

And Manjit said, 'Is too.'
And Lacey said, 'Is not.'
And Manjit said, 'Is too.'

And it went on like that for **LITERALLY** a whole minute (which I know because Manjit timed it) until I said I wasn't actually sure I fancied biscuits that had had monkey fingers on and maybe we should just report her to Mr Nidgett after all.

Only Lacey Braithwaite said in that case we would also have to report Harvey Barlow, who was busy eating discount biscuits behind the Poo Wagon (which is not actually a wagon made of poo,

it is the temporary boys' toilets,

because Manjit broke the real ones,

but that's another story).

Read more hilarious HIGH JINKS with
THE WORST CLASS IN THE WORLD

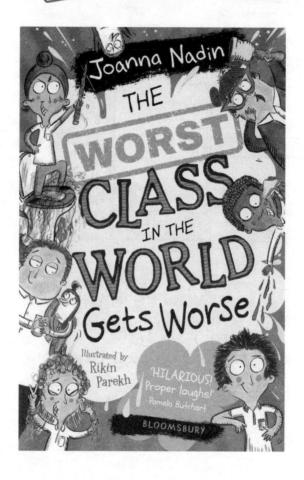

Guess what happens when Stanley and Manjit want to become the best playground monitors EVER and when they rescue a penguin from the zoo ...

WARNING: Contains flooding toilets, fish-finger-and-pickle sandwiches and penguin poop!

Read more hilarious HIGH JINKS with
THE WORST CLASS IN THE WORLD

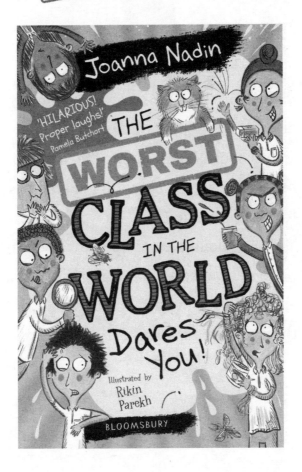

You won't believe what happens when 4B tries to catch NITS and to beat each other at DARES!

WARNING: Contains flying minibeasts, pooey pond water and really stinky burps!

Joanna Nadin is an award-winning author who has written more than eighty books for children. She has also been a juggler, a lifeguard and an adviser to the Prime Minister. The worst thing she ever did at school was be sick on her plate at lunch and blame it on someone else. She lives in Bath and her favourite things are goats, monkeys and crisps.

Rikin Parekh (aka Mr Rik) is an author/illustrator and ninja. He also works in primary schools as an LSA and worked as a bookseller (which was REALLY, REALLY fun!). The worst thing he ever did at school was to draw all over his exercise books (and in the margins!) and then get a big telling off for it! He lives in Wembley and his favourite things are pizza, dogs, and picking his nose and collecting the bogeys.